Penny and Peter

BOOKS BY CAROLYN HAYWOOD

"B" Is for Betsy
Betsy and Billy
Back to School with Betsy
Betsy and the Boys

Here's a Penny
Penny and Peter
Primrose Day
Two and Two Are Four

Penny and Peter

Carolyn Haywood

Illustrated by the author

AN ODYSSEY/HARCOURT YOUNG CLASSIC

HARCOURT, INC.

Orlando   Austin   New York   San Diego   Toronto   London

www.HarcourtBooks.com

First Odyssey/Harcourt Young Classics edition 2005
First published 1946

Library of Congress Cataloging-in-Publication Data
Haywood, Carolyn, 1898–1990.
Penny and Peter/written and illustrated by Carolyn Haywood.
p.   cm.
"An Odyssey/Harcourt Young Classic."
Summary: Whenever Penny and his adopted brother
Peter decide to help their parents, they usually end up in trouble.
[1. Brothers—Fiction. 2. Family life—Fiction.]   I. Title.
PZ7.H31496Pe   2005
[Fic]—dc22   2004059914
ISBN 0-15-205232-1   ISBN 0-15-205226-7 (pb)

Text set in Bodoni Classico
Designed by Kaelin Chappell

Printed in the United States of America

A C E G H F D B
A C E G H F D B (pb)

To
Blanche Ferry Hooker
and
Queene Ferry Coonley

CONTENTS

Penny and Peter

1

Crabs, Crabs, Beautiful Crabs

Penny's father and mother had adopted Penny when he was a tiny baby. They had waited for him a long time but when they found Penny, he was exactly what they wanted. They named him William but they called him Penny because his curly hair was just the color of a brand-new copper penny.

When Penny was six years old, he started to

go to school. There he met Peter who was eight. He was the best baseball player in the school. Peter lived in a children's orphanage because he didn't have any father or mother. The two boys were so fond of each other that Penny's father and mother took Peter to the seashore with them for the summer. At the end of the summer, they decided to adopt Peter. So, when the summer vacation was over and it was time to return home, the two little boys knew that they were going to be really truly brothers.

"Really truly brothers for ever and ever," said Penny.

Mother and Daddy had decided to leave the seashore the week after Labor Day but Daddy had to make an unexpected business trip so he had to leave the day after Labor Day.

Before he left, he put the sailboat away for the winter. Then he packed the car full of things that Mother said had to go back to town. When he finally drove off, there was nothing left for Mother and the boys to bring home on the train, along with Minnie, the cook, but one suitcase and the little traveling bag in which Really and Truly traveled. Really and Truly were

Penny's kittens but by this time they had grown into two very handsome cats.

"It's a great relief to have Daddy drive all of those things home," said Mother. "I would much rather go in the train. It is more comfortable than riding in the car with my feet in a pail and the floor mop hitting me on the head every time we turn a corner."

"Do you remember last year," asked Penny, "when Daddy stopped suddenly and the basket of tomatoes upset just as I slid off the seat?"

"I certainly do," said Mother. "And you landed right on top of those beautiful tomatoes. And was I angry!"

"And did we have tomato juice!" cried Penny. "It was all over everything, wasn't it, Mother?"

"It certainly was," said Mother. "But mostly all over you and the floor of the car."

Penny laughed as he recalled the mess he had suddenly found himself in, with all those tomatoes.

"We can laugh about it now," said Mother, "but it didn't seem very funny when it happened. This year, there will be nothing like that. We'll have a nice, quiet, peaceful trip home on the train."

"When are we leaving?" asked Peter.

"Next Monday," replied Mother. "We will go up on the two o'clock train. That will get us home before the rush hour."

Monday morning, after the boys had had their breakfast, they wandered around the house. They didn't seem to know what to do with themselves.

"Seems funny not to have the sailboat, doesn't it?" said Peter, as the boys sat on the dock swinging their feet.

"Seems 'though we ought to go out in a boat the very last day," said Penny.

"We could go out in the rowboat," said Peter.

"All right, let's!" said Penny. "And let's catch some crabs and surprise Minnie. It would be nice to take some crabs home with us. Don't you think so, Peter?"

"Yes," said Peter. "I love crabs. And we won't get any more until next summer."

"Well then, we'll have to catch a fish for bait," said Penny.

Penny ran to the garage to get their fishing tackle, while Peter hunted for a clam to use for fish bait.

In a short time, the boys were settled on the

end of the dock each with his line in the water.
They were as quiet as two statues.

Then Peter began to pull his line. He didn't
jerk it but pulled it in carefully.

"I've got one," he whispered to Penny.

Penny looked down into the water. Sure
enough, there on the end of Peter's line was a
good-sized fish. It was fighting hard but Peter

knew how to handle his line and he landed the fish, flip-flapping, onto the dock.

Ten minutes later, Peter and Penny were out in the rowboat with half of the fish fastened to Penny's line and the other half fastened to Peter's. They sat motionless a long time, staring into the water.

"Don't seem to be any crabs this morning," said Penny.

"Sometimes they come along all at once," said Peter.

"I know," said Penny. "But sometimes you have to go someplace else."

"Well, let's wait a little longer," said Peter. They sat waiting.

All of a sudden, Peter picked up the net and scooped down into the water.

"Got one!" he said, as he lifted the net. "A great big one."

"Me, too!" said Penny. "Quick, Peter, get it."

Peter emptied his crab out of the net into the basket that the boys had placed in the center of the rowboat. Then he scooped up the crab that was busy nibbling away at the fish on the end of Penny's line.

Suddenly, the water around the boat was full

of crabs. Peter scooped them up, one after another, as fast as he could. In no time at all, the boys had caught about fifty crabs.

"Aren't they beauts!" cried Peter.

"They're the biggest crabs I have ever seen," said Penny.

Peter looked across the water toward the house on the cliff. Then he said, "Lunch is ready. Minnie has put the signal out."

At mealtimes, Minnie always hung an old red sweater on the clothesline. This was the signal to come home.

"Well, we made a good haul," said Penny, as Peter began pulling on the oars.

When the boat was secured to the dock, the boys lifted the basket of crabs out of the boat.

"They're lively critters, aren't they?" said Peter, watching the big green crabs.

"They sure are the biggest crabs we've caught all summer. They must all be granddaddies," said Penny.

The boys carried the basket between them to the back door.

"Look, Minnie!" cried Penny. "Look at the beautiful crabs we caught."

"Crabs!" cried Minnie. "What made you

catch crabs? What are we going to do with crabs when we're going home on the two o'clock train?" Minnie came to open the screen door to let the boys in.

"Goodness!" she cried. "All those crabs! How many have you got there?"

"About fifty," said Peter.

"Fifty crabs!" cried Minnie. "Fifty crabs, and we're going home on the two o'clock train."

"But they're beautiful crabs, Minnie," said Penny. "You never saw such beautiful crabs. Look how big they are."

"I'm looking at them," said Minnie. "But

what I want to know is what you're going to do with them."

Just then, Mother came into the kitchen.

"Look, Mother!" cried Penny. "Look at the beautiful crabs we caught."

"But what are we going to do with them?" asked Mother.

"That's just what I want to know," said Minnie.

"We can take them home with us," said Peter. "They will be all right in this basket. We can put more seaweed over them. They'll be all right in the train. And I love crabs."

"So do I," said Penny.

Minnie grunted. Then she said, "Come along. Lunch is getting cold. Never know what you boys will bring into the house."

"Well, the boys will have to carry the basket of crabs," said Mother. "In fact, they will have to take full charge of them. Minnie and I have enough to take care of."

"Okay!" said Penny. "We'll take care of them, won't we, Peter?"

"Sure!" said Peter.

Mother had the one remaining suitcase packed and Minnie had a large black leather bag and a shopping bag. In the shopping bag she had odds and ends. It was filled with half-empty packages of flour, cocoa, sugar, cornstarch, and raisins—things that Minnie would use up when they got back home. Also, into the shopping bag went Minnie's favorite gadgets, such as the can opener, knife sharpener, and apple corer. Sticking out of the bag were the long handles of the pancake turner and the soup ladle. The bag was sitting on the kitchen chair when Mother came out into the kitchen after lunch.

"Why are you taking the pancake turner and the soup ladle, Minnie? We have others at home," said Mother.

"Well, I just got awful fond of them," said Minnie. "Somehow, I think I'm going to need them. The pancake turner's nice and limber and the soup ladle's not too big."

Finally, the taxi was at the door to take them to the train.

Penny put Really and Truly into their traveling bag. There was a great deal of mewing as Penny placed the bag in the taxi. Then Peter and Penny carried the basket of crabs out and put it in the taxi.

"You boys are sure there is plenty of seaweed in the basket with the crabs, aren't you?" asked Mother.

"Oh! Sure, sure!" said Peter. "We put in a lot of seaweed, and the crabs are very quiet."

"Well, that's good," said Mother, as she climbed into the taxi. "Here's hoping they keep quiet!"

Minnie, with her bags, climbed in beside the taxi driver.

"I've traveled with lots of things in my day," said Minnie, "but this is the first time I've traveled with fifty crabs."

"But they're beautiful crabs, Minnie," said Penny.

"Oh, sure, sure! They're beautiful crabs," said Minnie. "I just hope they take a nice long nap on the train and don't get into trouble."

"What trouble could they get into?" asked Peter. "They're so quiet you wouldn't know they were in the basket." And then, as a shuffling sound came from the basket, Peter added, "Almost."

"Well, I just hope for the best," said Minnie. "I just hope for the best."

This made Mother laugh and she said, "Oh,

Minnie! Don't be so gloomy about the crabs. They are quite all right in the basket."

Minnie sighed. "I just hope for the best," she said.

When they reached the station, the train was rapidly filling with passengers. Mother carried the suitcase in one hand and Really and Truly in the other. The boys carried the basket of crabs between them and Minnie brought up the rear with her black bag and the shopping bag.

Carrying the basket of crabs up the steep steps of the car was not easy, but the boys managed it slowly.

Mother led the way to four vacant seats that faced each other in the center of the car. The suitcase she stowed away on the rack overhead. The bag containing Really and Truly she placed on the floor.

"Now, boys," she said, "you will have to put the basket of crabs between the seats and do the best you can with your feet and legs. After all, the crabs were your idea."

"Okay!" said Peter, as the boys reached the seat. "Put it down, Penny."

Penny dropped his end of the basket so suddenly that it startled Peter, and before you could say "Boo!" the basket of crabs had tipped over and nearly all the crabs and the seaweed lay sprawling in the aisle.

The excited crabs began scrambling in all directions. Women and children, nearby, jumped up on the seats to get out of the way of the pinching crabs. The children yelled and squealed. The aisle was blocked and people couldn't get through. When they saw the crabs scurrying around in the aisle and under the seats, they fled out of the doors of the car.

Minnie started to cry, "Goodness! Goodness!"

Peter righted the basket while Penny jumped up and down and cried, "Oh, Mummy! Oh, Mummy! Oh, Mummy!"

"Be quiet, Penny. Minnie, stop yelling and do something," said Mother. "Here, give me the pancake turner."

Mother pulled the pancake turner out of the shopping bag and went after a nearby crab. She scooped for it but it slid right off. Meanwhile, the other crabs were getting farther and farther away. Everyone in the car was either kneeling or standing on the seats and they were all watching the crabs.

"Oh, dear!" said Mother. "This will never do. Here, give me the soup ladle."

Minnie handed over the soup ladle. With the

pancake turner under the crab and the soup ladle pinning it down on top, Mother was able to lift one crab back into the basket. And then, the crabs in the basket started such a commotion as their fellow crab returned. Mother went after another.

By this time, most of the crabs had hidden under the seats. They could be heard scratching their claws on the floor.

"I think I can get them, Mother," said Peter. "I can get under the seats more easily."

Meanwhile, Minnie had gathered up the seaweed. She kept muttering over and over, "I never did trust crabs. They're just plain wicked."

The aisle was now cleared of everything but Peter and Penny, who went crawling up and down looking for crabs. Peter had the pancake turner in one hand and the soup ladle in the other. Every once in a while he would chase a crab out from under a seat, put the pancake turner under it, the soup ladle on top of it, and drop it into the basket. Many a time he dropped the crab and had to begin over again, but by the time the train had gone halfway home, all of the wandering crabs had been caught and were safely back in the basket. They had settled down under the seaweed.

Once, Penny looked down at the basket and said, "I'm glad we didn't lose the crabs, aren't you, Mummy?"

"Well," replied Mother, "it would have been better to have left them in the ocean."

"Oh, but Mother," said Penny, "they are such beautiful crabs!"

"Beautiful crabs!" muttered Minnie. "Just full of meanness, that's what. Nothing beautiful about them."

At the end of the journey, Mother asked the conductor if he would lift the basket off the train. Peter and Penny carried it safely to a taxicab.

At last they reached home and Mother and Minnie breathed a sigh of relief.

"I won't trust those crabs until I get them in the pot," said Minnie. And without taking off her hat, she put a big kettle of water on the stove.

When the water was boiling, she threw the crabs in one by one. As she did so, she muttered to herself, "Beautiful crabs! I just hope I never travel again with crabs. The most awful good-for-nothing nuisance in the world is a crab."

When they were done, Minnie laid the big fat crabs out on the kitchen table. Penny came into the kitchen. Minnie stood back and admired the crabs. Then a broad grin spread over her face. "My! Oh, my, Penny!" she said. "Aren't they beautiful crabs?"

2

How to Paint a Floor

Peter's bedroom was next to Penny's room. Before Peter came to live at Penny's house, it had been the guest room. As it didn't look very much like a boy's room, Daddy decided to do the whole room over.

"I saw a wonderful red, white, and blue wallpaper the other day," said Daddy. "And we will paint the floor a nice shade of blue."

"And we can use a red bedspread and white curtains," said Mother.

So, in no time at all, Daddy had moved everything out of the room. Peter was to sleep on the daybed in the upstairs study until the room was finished.

The paper hangers came and hung the red, white, and blue wallpaper and Daddy bought the blue paint to paint the floor.

A few days before school opened, Mother went into town to do some shopping. It was Minnie's day out and the two boys were left alone.

Before Mother left, she said, "How would you boys like to meet Daddy and me this evening for dinner and go to a movie?"

"Great!" cried Peter.

"Swell!" said Penny.

Mother told them the name of the restaurant.

"Oh, I know where that is," said Peter. "I used to serve papers there when I had my paper route."

"Very well," said Mother. "You and Penny be there at six o'clock sharp."

"All right, Mother," said Peter.

After Mother left, the boys looked around for something to do. They wandered into the room that was to be Peter's. By the door, in the empty room, sat a large can of blue paint and a package containing two large paintbrushes. Peter walked over and examined the can.

"I heard Daddy say that he wished the floor was painted," said Peter. "I wonder if we could paint it and surprise him when he gets home."

"Oh, I like to paint," said Penny. "I just love to paint."

"Well, let's do it," said Peter.

The boys squatted down beside the can of paint and Peter unwrapped the package of paintbrushes.

"I helped paint a floor once when I lived at the orphanage," said Peter.

"You know how to do lots of things, don't you, Peter?" said Penny.

"Pretty many," said Peter, as he went off to get a screwdriver to lift the lid off the can of paint.

When he returned he had a screwdriver and a sturdy stick. He pried off the lid and thrust the stick into the can.

"You have to stir it until it is smooth," he said, as he began to stir the paint round and round with the stick.

At first, it was very hard to stir, but the more he stirred the easier it became. And the color grew more beautiful.

Penny sat on the floor beside Peter. While Peter stirred, the two boys talked. "Do you know Jimmy and Jackie Landon?" asked Penny.

"Sure!" said Peter. "They're in your room in school, aren't they?"

"Yes," replied Penny. "And do you know what Jimmy and Jackie have in their bedroom?"

"What?" asked Peter.

"They have bunk beds," answered Penny. "Do you know what bunk beds are?"

"Sure," said Peter. "They're like the beds on trains. One is down low and the other is up high, near the ceiling."

"And you climb up a ladder to get into the upper one," said Penny.

"That's right," said Peter.

"I wish we had bunk beds," said Penny.

"I read a story once about some people who had a cabin in the woods. They had bunk beds," said Peter.

"They did?" said Penny. "They had a cabin in the woods?"

"Yepper!" replied Peter. "And it was an exciting story."

"Were there wild animals in the woods?" asked Penny.

"Oh, sure!" said Peter.

"Would you like a cabin in the woods?" asked Penny.

"You bet!" replied Peter. "Someday, I'm going to have one."

"Would you be afraid of the wild animals?" asked Penny.

"'Course not," said Peter.

"Wouldn't you even be afraid of a wolf?" asked Penny.

"No," replied Peter. "I would shoot it. Would you be afraid?"

"No," answered Penny. "I wouldn't be afraid of any old wolf."

"Well, then, you can stay in my cabin when I get it," said Peter. "You can sleep in one of the bunks."

Penny looked into the can of paint. "Isn't it done yet?" he asked.

"Almost," Peter answered.

At last, Peter said, "Now it's ready." And just then, he tipped the can and spilled some of the paint on the floor. Peter picked up one of the brushes and spread the paint that had been spilled. "We might as well begin right here," he said.

Penny was delighted to finally dip his brush in the paint. He liked spreading the blue paint over the floorboards. He watched Peter and tried to do it just the way he did.

Peter was so much interested in what he was doing that he didn't notice that when he began with the spilled paint, it was right in front of the only door in the room. He just painted and painted and painted. And Penny painted and painted and painted. Every once in a while they moved the bucket of paint and they got farther and farther away from the door. Before very long there was a strip of blue paint from one wall to the other. It was so wide that no one could have stepped over it—not even Daddy, with his long legs. But they never noticed that the only way out was getting farther and farther away from them. They were too busy painting. Occasionally, they would sit back and admire their work.

Once Peter said, "It looks swell, doesn't it?"

"Yes," replied Penny. "Won't Daddy be surprised?"

And then, in the doorway, Truly, Penny's black cat with white paws, appeared.

"Don't come in, Truly," shouted Penny. "Don't come in!"

Truly put his white nose down and wiped up some paint. He looked so funny when he lifted his face. He was wearing blue lipstick. Peter and Penny screamed with laughter.

Then Truly lifted one white paw. He was just about to put it down on the blue paint when Peter cried, "Scat!"

Truly was so surprised, he turned tail and fled down the stairs, taking his little blue nose with him.

The boys set to work again. By this time, there was a good deal of paint on their hands, and their overalls were pretty well spotted. They went on painting.

Then Really, Penny's yellow cat, appeared in the doorway. "Scat!" cried Penny. "Go away," he cried, as Really showed signs of walking right over the blue paint.

Peter reached into his pocket and pulled out a wad of paper. He threw it as hard as he could at Really. Really was so frightened that he turned suddenly and he swept the blue paint with his long yellow tail. The last the boys saw of Really was his tail, waving like a paintbrush dipped in blue.

The boys sighed in relief. "I thought he was surely going to spoil the floor," said Peter.

"We don't want anything to spoil it," said Penny, as they set to work again.

The room wasn't very large, so by the time the church clock struck five, they were just about half finished.

"Pretty soon, we'll have to get washed and dressed to go meet Mother and Daddy," said Peter.

"Yes," said Penny. "I guess we won't get it all finished, will we?"

"I guess not," replied Peter.

"Won't Daddy be surprised?" said Penny.

"He'll be surprised good," said Peter, finishing another board. Then he sat back on his heels. He looked at the open door as though for the first time. Then he looked behind him at the wall with the windows. Then he said, "S-a-a-a-ay, Penny!"

Penny looked up with his eyes big and round. "What is it?" he asked.

"Look!" said Peter.

"Where?" said Penny.

"At the door," said Peter.

Penny looked. "What's the matter with it?" he asked.

"Look where it is," said Peter. "How are we going to get out?"

Penny's eyes grew larger and larger as he looked at the lake of blue paint that lay between them and the door. Finally he said, "Well, what will we do?"

"We don't want to walk on it," said Peter.

Peter went to the window and looked out.

The ground looked very far away. The church clock struck half past five. "It's half past five," he said. "Mother said to leave at half past five."

"We could take off our shoes and stockings," said Penny, "and tiptoe to the door."

"We would mess it up, 'cause it's awfully slippery," said Peter, gloomily.

"Well, what shall we do?" asked Penny.

Just then, a voice called from downstairs, "Yoo-hoo! Penny!"

"Hi! Patsy!" Penny called back. "Come on up."

Footsteps came stamping up the stairs and in a moment, Patsy, the little girl who lived next door, appeared.

"What are you doing?" she asked.

"We've been painting the floor," said Penny. "And now we can't get out of the room without walking on the paint."

"Oh!" said Patsy.

"And we have to meet Mother and Daddy at six o'clock," said Peter.

"Oh!" cried Patsy. "You will have to climb out of the window. Isn't it exciting? I wish I were over there and had to climb out of the window. I like to climb out of windows, but Mummy doesn't like me to do it."

"We can't climb out of the window," said Peter, impatiently. "How could we, when it's so high?"

"Oh!" said Patsy. "I thought the porch roof was there. Wouldn't it be nice if the porch roof was there? I like to sit on the porch roof. One day I sat on the porch roof all afternoon and nobody knew where I was. But Mummy didn't like it. I got my dress awfully dirty."

"Oh, Patsy!" interrupted Peter. "Don't just stand there talking. Do something."

"What shall I do?" Patsy asked.

"Oh, I guess we will just have to walk on it," said Peter.

"If you had a bridge, you could walk across the bridge," said Patsy.

"Is that so?" said Peter. "And where are we going to get a bridge?"

"Well, it's an awfully good idea," said Patsy.

"Oh, come on, Peter," said Penny. "We'll have to walk on it."

"Do you have a ladder?" asked Patsy.

"Yes," replied Peter, "but it isn't long enough to reach to the window."

"Maybe you could make a bridge out of it," said Patsy.

Peter looked at Patsy and his eyes opened very wide. "Maybe we could," he said. "You go down to the garage and bring it up, Patsy."

Patsy ran down to the garage. After some time she returned, dragging the ladder. She had quite a time bringing it upstairs, but she finally landed it outside of the bedroom door.

"Now," said Peter, "there are two little stools in Mother's room. Get them and throw one of them in here to me."

Patsy went off for the stools and reappeared with one in each hand.

"Now, throw it far enough so that it won't land in the paint," said Peter.

Patsy flung the stool with all of her might. Peter, being an expert catcher, caught it. He placed it on the unpainted part of the floor.

"Now, stand the ladder up straight," said Peter. "And let it come down gently. Don't drop it."

Patsy held the ladder up straight. Then she tipped it toward the inside of the room. Suddenly it dropped, but Peter was quick and caught the end of the ladder. He just saved it from landing on the paint.

"Now, put your stool under your end," said Peter.

Patsy slipped her stool under the end of the ladder and Peter placed the other stool under his end. "That's great!" he said. "Now, go ahead, Penny. You go across, first."

Penny stepped on the first rung of the ladder, then to the second and then to the next, until he reached the end. Peter followed.

"Didn't I tell you a bridge was a good idea?" said Patsy.

"It was great," replied Peter, as he dashed off to wash his hands.

"We won't have time to change our clothes," he called to Penny. "We're late now."

Patsy ran home to her dinner and Penny washed his hands. Then the two boys set out on a run to meet Daddy and Mother. They ran all the way. When they reached the restaurant, Daddy was standing out on the pavement looking for them.

"What made you so late?" he said, when the boys arrived.

"We were doing something," said Penny. "It's a surprise for you, Daddy."

"And we got sorta stuck," said Penny. "We didn't have time to change our clothes."

"So I see," said Daddy.

When Mother saw the boys in their overalls, she, too, was surprised. "Why, boys!" she said. "Why didn't you get dressed?"

"We couldn't," said Peter. "We were so late. We thought you would be worried."

"We were making a surprise for Daddy," said Penny. "And we got sort of stuck."

When they were all seated at the table, Daddy looked at the boys' overalls and at the blue stains on their hands. Then he looked across the table at Mother. "You know, Mother, I have been thinking. I think perhaps it would be nicer to paint the floor of Peter's room red."

Penny and Peter sat bolt upright and stared at each other, their eyes popping.

"Red!" cried Mother.

"Yes," said Daddy. "A nice bright red."

"Oh no, Daddy!" cried Penny. "Not red!"

"Oh no! Not red," said Peter. "You wouldn't like it red, Daddy."

"Well, maybe not," said Daddy. "I guess I had better use that nice blue paint that I bought."

Peter and Penny looked across the table at each other and grinned. Penny wriggled, he was so pleased. Then he said, "I think you will like it, Daddy."

3

Tootsie

For a long time, Patsy had wanted a dog. "A nice little dog," Patsy would say. "I want a nice little dog. Not one like that wirehaired terrier that lives down the street. I want a nice quiet doggie."

When Patsy said this to her daddy, he would say, "Well, perhaps someday." And when she chattered about the dog to her mother, she would say, "Well, we'll see."

Patsy was beginning to feel that Daddy's "someday" would never come and that Mummy would never "see" when a letter arrived from her uncle Frank. Uncle Frank lived out west. He wrote that he was going into the army and he didn't know what to do with his dog "Tootsie." Would they like to have her, and if they wanted her, send a telegram.

Patsy was so excited, she hopped up and down on one foot, saying over and over, "Sure we'll take her. Sure we'll take her. Won't we, Daddy? Won't we?"

So her daddy sent the telegram to Uncle Frank. He said that they would be glad to take Tootsie.

"What kind of dog do you suppose Tootsie is?" said Patsy.

"I don't know," said her daddy. "As long as it isn't one of those Pekingese that expect to lie on a pillow all day, I don't care. Tootsie sounds very much like a Pekingese. They yap, too."

"Maybe it's a little cocker spaniel," said Patsy. "I just love cocker spaniels."

"I don't care what kind it is," said Patsy's mother, "just as long as it is little. And the littler the better."

"You're not hoping for a Mexican hairless!" cried her daddy. "They look like some kind of bug."

"No," laughed Mrs. Sawyer. "It doesn't have to be that little."

When Patsy saw Penny, she said, "Oh, Penny! What do you think! I'm going to get a dog. My uncle Frank is sending it. Its name is Tootsie."

"That's fine," said Penny. "What kind is it?"

"I don't know yet," said Patsy. "Some kind of a little dog. Maybe a cocker spaniel or maybe a Scottie or maybe one of those little white ones with hair hanging over its eyes. I don't know what you call them."

"You mean a poodle," said Peter, who had joined the children. "They look like floor mops."

"Yes," said Patsy. "That's it. A poodle."

"Are you going to build a doghouse for it?" Penny asked.

"Oh no!" replied Patsy. "Tootsie is going to sleep in my room. Daddy and I are going to buy a little bed for her and it's going to be right beside my bed."

Patsy talked of nothing but Tootsie. For days, it was, "Daddy, when are we going to buy Tootsie's bed? Mummy, when do you think

Tootsie will come?" Then, after a while, it was, "Daddy, do you think Tootsie will come today?"

One Saturday afternoon, her daddy took her to a department store. They went to the sporting goods department where all kinds of things for dogs could be found. They walked around until they came upon a pile of wicker beds.

"What size bed are you interested in?" asked the salesman.

"Oh, a small one," said Mr. Sawyer. "It is for a little dog."

The salesman pulled out one of the beds. "This should be all right," he said. "We sell these for small dogs. Plenty big enough for a cocker or a Scottie."

"Yes," said Mr. Sawyer. "That should be about right."

Patsy thought it was a lovely little bed, with its bright green cushion.

"Is there anything else, sir?" asked the salesman.

"Oh, Daddy!" cried Patsy. "Look at the darling little bowls for the doggie's food. Can't we buy Tootsie a little bowl?"

Daddy looked at the bowls. Now Patsy had found some double ones, for food and water. "Oh, Daddy!" she cried. "Look at these!"

"They are very nice," said the salesman. "Won't tip over and small enough so that the ears will hang down, outside of the bowl. Plenty large enough, too, for one feeding for a small dog."

"Very well," said Mr. Sawyer. "Let's have one of those."

"How about a leash?" said the salesman. "We have some very nice leashes over here." He led the way to a rack from which hung a bunch of leashes. He took one down. "This is a nice leash for a Scottie," he said. "What kind of dog did you say yours is?"

"As a matter of fact," said Mr. Sawyer, "we

don't know. She is being shipped to us from the west. She is some kind of small dog."

"Oh, Daddy!" said Patsy. "I think the plaid leash is so pretty, and maybe she is a Scottie."

"Well," said Daddy, "we'll take the leash. But I hope she doesn't turn out to be a dachshund."

A few days later, word came from Uncle Frank that Tootsie had been shipped. Patsy ran right to the grocery store to buy a box of dog biscuits.

"Do you want the regular dog biscuits," said the grocer, "or do you want puppy biscuits?"

"I don't know," said Patsy. "They are for a little dog."

"Puppy biscuits," said the grocer, lifting a box from the shelf. Patsy paid for it and trotted home with the box under her arm. She loved the pictures on the box. On one side there was a picture of a sad-looking cocker spaniel. On the other, a perky-looking Scottie.

"Oh, Mummy!" Patsy sighed. "Do you think Tootsie will look like either of these doggies?"

"I don't know, dear," said her mother. "Don't get your heart set on any one kind, because you might be disappointed."

"Oh, I won't be disappointed," said Patsy. "I

don't care what kind of dog Tootsie is, just so she isn't like that wirehaired terrier that lives down the street. I love every dog 'cept him. He chases everything. He chases me and he chases automobiles and he chases Really and Truly. Tootsie won't be like that. I know that Tootsie will be a good quiet dog. And I'll take her on my lap and hold her. And I'll brush her hair and I'll cover her up every night with my doll's blanket. And she'll trot along beside me when I take her out walking. And I'll give her a bath in my doll's washtub."

One evening, the telephone bell rang and when Mr. Sawyer answered it, a voice said, "Mr. Sawyer, this is the railway station. We have a dog down here in the baggage room for you. She just came in by Railway Express. Our trucks don't go out on deliveries again until tomorrow. Thought you might like to come down and get her. Don't want her barking here all night."

"Oh, thanks very much," said Mr. Sawyer. "I'll be right down."

Patsy was so excited when she heard the news that she ran around in circles. "Can I go with you, Daddy?" she cried. "I can go with you to get Tootsie, can't I?"

"Yes, of course you can go," said her daddy.

She was so excited, she forgot to put her coat on.

"Here! Patsy!" her mother called after her. "Come back and put your coat and hat on."

"Oh yes!" said Patsy. "I forgot."

She ran back into the house and put on the coat that her mother was holding. She put her hat on backward.

"Oh, Mummy!" she said. "Just think! Tootsie's at the station! I can hold her on my lap all the way home."

Patsy dashed off again and climbed into the car beside her father. He started the car and off they went. But, just as they turned out of the drive, Patsy cried, "Oh, Daddy! Wait! Wait! I forgot something."

Mr. Sawyer stopped the car. "Now what?" he said. But Patsy was already out of the car and running as fast as her legs would go.

When she burst into the house, her mother cried, "Now what?"

"I forgot Tootsie's leash," Patsy called, running to the coat closet.

She lifted the plaid leash off the hook and ran back to the car. "I forgot her leash," she said to her daddy as she climbed in again.

Mr. Sawyer started off once more. It wasn't long before they reached the railway station. Mr. Sawyer jumped out of the car and Patsy followed with the little plaid leash. Her daddy went into the station and walked over to the window to speak to the station agent. "I came for the dog," Mr. Sawyer said.

"Oh, sure!" replied the agent. "The dog. She's out in the baggage room. I suppose you want to take her out of the crate?"

"Oh, yes," replied Mr. Sawyer. "I brought some tools to unfasten it."

"Good," said the station agent, leading the way to the baggage room. "She's some dog, Mr. Sawyer!"

"Is that so?" said Mr. Sawyer.

Suddenly, a terrific sound burst forth. It was like a lion roaring. Patsy jumped. "What under the sun is that?" cried her daddy.

"That's her," said the station agent.

"Jumping grasshoppers!" cried Mr. Sawyer.

The station agent put his key in the door. "I thought sure they were bringing in a piano when that crate arrived," he said.

"What do you mean, 'a piano'?" cried Mr. Sawyer.

The station agent kicked the door open. "Say!" he said. "Haven't you seen this dog?"

"No, I haven't," said Mr. Sawyer. "All we know is that her name is Tootsie."

"Tootsie!" shouted the station agent. "Well, here she is."

Patsy and her daddy looked at the enormous crate and there, standing up inside, was the biggest dog Patsy had ever seen. Tootsie was a Great Dane.

Mr. Sawyer and Patsy were both speechless. They just stared at the enormous creature.

Tootsie wagged her tail. Then, suddenly, she said, "Woof!" and Patsy grabbed her hat. She thought it was going to blow right off.

They stood looking at Tootsie for some time. At last Patsy said, "I guess her bed won't fit her, Daddy. But she can sleep in mine."

4

There's a Dog in My Chair

Daddy set to work to open Tootsie's crate. The station agent helped and it wasn't long before Tootsie was free. Her bark turned into happy yelps that sounded like a sea lion. She wagged her huge tail and her red tongue looked almost a foot long.

Patsy stood very close to her daddy, for Tootsie looked awfully big and fierce.

"Now, don't be afraid of her," said Mr. Sawyer. "She won't hurt you. But, my goodness gracious! Where are we going to keep her?"

Tootsie looked at Mr. Sawyer and her mouth widened.

Patsy let out a scream.

"Now, see here," said her daddy, "you wanted a dog, didn't you?"

"Yes," said Patsy. "But she is so much dog. I thought she was going to be a little dog."

"Well, if you don't like her," said Daddy, "we will send her to a kennel and pay her board."

Tootsie pulled in her tongue and closed her great mouth. Suddenly, she looked sad. It was as though she understood every word that was spoken.

"Now, you've hurt her feelings," Patsy murmured.

"Well, pat her and make her feel better," said Mr. Sawyer.

Patsy put her hand out and patted Tootsie's head. Immediately, she looked pleased. In another moment, Patsy's arms were around the dog's neck. Tootsie's tail hit the packing boxes with loud whacks.

"That's right," said her daddy, "you make her

45

feel welcome. I am afraid she is in for a cold reception when she gets home. Your mother said, 'The littler the better,' and I am afraid that means, 'The bigger the worser.' Come on, let's get it over."

Tootsie sat in the back seat of the car looking very pleased and Patsy sat beside her looking very little.

Soon they turned into the drive and the car stopped.

"Now, I think we had better break this to your mother gently," said Patsy's daddy. "You wait here with Tootsie."

Mr. Sawyer left Patsy and the dog in the car and went into the house.

"So, you're back!" called Mrs. Sawyer from the living room. "Well, where's Tootsie? Where's Patsy?"

"They'll be in in a moment," said Mr. Sawyer.

"What is the matter?" asked Mrs. Sawyer, standing up. "Is anything the matter?"

"No, no!" said Mr. Sawyer. "Not a thing. It's just that—"

Suddenly, there was a terrific bump on the front door.

"What is that?" cried Mrs. Sawyer, starting toward the front door.

"Wait a minute!" cried Mr. Sawyer, hurrying after her.

"What is the matter with you?" asked Mrs. Sawyer.

Bang! Thump! There was the noise at the front door again.

Mrs. Sawyer pulled the door open and Tootsie bounded into the hall. Inside of the house, Tootsie looked bigger than ever. She looked as big as a pony.

"Good grief!" cried Patsy's mother, as Tootsie galloped into the living room. "Is this Tootsie?"

"That's her," said Mr. Sawyer.

"Didn't Daddy tell you how big Tootsie is?" asked Patsy.

"No," replied Mother, "he never got round to telling me. I just knew that he had something on his mind."

"I didn't have time," said her daddy.

"But what will we do with a dog like that?" said her mother, as the family followed Tootsie into the living room. To their great surprise, Tootsie was nowhere in sight.

"Where did she go?" cried Patsy.

"Why, how strange!" exclaimed her mother.

They looked in the dining room and behind all of the furniture. Patsy even looked under the davenport, although Tootsie could no more have squeezed under the davenport than an elephant.

And then, Mrs. Sawyer noticed that the door onto the side porch was open. The draperies were drawn across the opening and it didn't show.

"Why, she must have gone out of this door!" said Mrs. Sawyer. "Now, how do you suppose she knew that it was open?"

"Just smelled the fresh air, I suppose," said

Mr. Sawyer. "I'll see if I can find her. It is so terribly dark. There isn't any moon."

"I'll come with you," said Patsy.

"No, you stay here with Mother," said her daddy. "I can look better by myself. I don't want to have to look for you as well as the dog."

"It is past your bedtime, Patsy," said her mother. "We'll go upstairs and get you tucked into bed."

"But I can't go to sleep until Daddy finds Tootsie," said Patsy, beginning to cry.

"Now, don't worry about Tootsie," said Mother. "You couldn't possibly lose anything as big as Tootsie. She will be back in no time. Daddy will have to build a separate house for her, I can see that. Tootsie! What a name for a Great Dane!"

Patsy went upstairs and her mother followed. It took Patsy a long time to get ready for bed because, every few minutes, she ran to look out of the window. There was no sign of Tootsie or Daddy. At last, she was tucked into bed and although she tried to stay awake until Tootsie came back, she was soon fast asleep.

Meanwhile, Mr. Sawyer hunted all over the neighborhood for the dog. She seemed to have melted away. After an hour, he came home and telephoned the police. They said that they would radio the police cars and that they would be on the lookout for a Great Dane.

The fact was, Tootsie had not gone far. She had galloped through the Sawyers' living room and out of the door, across the porch and across the drive that lay between Patsy's house and Penny's.

Penny's father had opened the front door to put out the milk bottles and had decided to walk around to the back of the house to see if the toolshed door was locked. He left the front door open and Tootsie walked in. She sniffed the rugs in the hall and she sniffed the carpet on the stairs. No one was around, for Peter and Penny and their mother had gone to bed.

Tootsie walked up the stairs. She sniffed around the upstairs hall. The door into Penny's room was open, so Tootsie walked in. She sniffed all around. She sniffed the bed. Penny was sound asleep. Tootsie turned around three times and lay down beside the bed. In a few moments, she, too, was sound asleep.

Penny's daddy came into the house and locked the front door. He put out the light on the hall table and climbed the stairs. He opened his bedroom door, went in, and closed the door behind him.

The house was quiet and dark. Everyone, including Tootsie, slept. But she didn't sleep very long. She woke up, thirsty and hungry. She got up and stretched her great body. Again, she sniffed around the room. Then she went into the hall. Silently, she padded down the carpeted stairs. She went into the dining room and sniffed her way to the kitchen door. She could smell chocolate cake and she liked chocolate cake.

With her great nose, Tootsie pushed the swinging door open. The cats' bowl of water stood under the sink. Tootsie lapped it all up. It wasn't a very big drink but it was better than none. Then she lifted her head and sniffed some more. She followed her nose to the kitchen table and the odor of chocolate cake grew stronger. She put her paws up on the table and looked right at a great big chocolate cake.

Minnie had made the cake but had not had time to ice it, so Penny's mother had iced the cake before she went to bed and left it on the table to set.

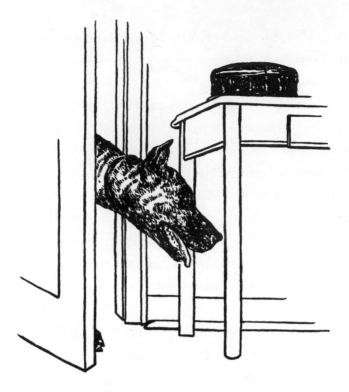

Tootsie stuck out her long tongue and took a great lick of chocolate icing. It was good. It was so good that Tootsie went back for more. Only this time, she took a great big bite right out of the cake. She swallowed it down and took another bite. Half of the cake was gone. Two more bites and all that remained on the plate were crumbs and smears of chocolate icing.

Tootsie licked her chops and smacked her

lips. She felt much more comfortable inside. She pushed open the swinging door and made her way through the dining room, up the stairs and into Penny's room.

There was a big chair in Penny's room, almost as big as a couch. Tootsie jumped up on the chair, settled down, and went to sleep.

Toward morning, she woke up. Something was biting her. She lifted her hind leg and scratched. Her leg made a noise as it beat against the chair cushion.

Penny stirred in his sleep. He turned over and opened his eyes. A very faint light came through the window so that everything in the room showed dimly. Everything looked a little bit strange and unreal. Through his eyes, half closed with sleep, Penny looked at the big chair. He thought he saw a great big dog in the chair. The dog was asleep.

Penny began to feel scared. It looked like a dog in his chair but he didn't have a dog and he had never seen such a big dog before. He guessed he would go tell Daddy.

Very quietly, Penny crawled out of his bed. In his bare feet, he pattered over to the room where his mother and daddy slept. He opened

the door and in the dim light, reached the side of his daddy's bed.

"Daddy!" he whispered. "Daddy!"

Daddy grunted.

"Daddy!" whispered Penny, gently shaking Daddy's shoulder.

Daddy opened one eye. "What's the matter?" he whispered.

"There's a great big dog in my chair," said Penny.

"What's 'at?" said Daddy.

"I said, there's a great big dog in my room. It's the biggest dog I've ever seen. It's in my chair."

"You've been dreaming," said Daddy.

"No, I haven't, Daddy," said Penny. "There is a dog there. You come and look."

"There couldn't be a dog there, Penny," said Daddy. "We don't have a dog. Come on, get into my bed and go to sleep again. It's awfully early."

Penny liked nothing better than to get into bed with Daddy, so he climbed in. He put his head on his daddy's chest and felt the comfort of his daddy's big arms around him.

"You just had a dream," said Daddy.

"Well, I thought it was a real dog," said Penny, and he dozed off to sleep.

About an hour later, Tootsie woke up. The chocolate cake had made her thirsty. She couldn't stand it. She wanted a drink. She lifted her head and gave a terrific yelp. Daddy, Mother, Peter, and Penny all woke up with a start.

"What was that!" cried Mother.

Daddy was already out of the door, followed

by Penny. Peter met them as he ran out of his room. "What's the matter?" he cried.

Daddy led the way to Penny's room. There, in the clear morning light, was Tootsie, barking her head off. When she saw them, she wagged her great tail and let out a powerful "Woof!"

"Great snakes!" cried Daddy.

"I told you there was a dog, Daddy," said Penny. "Didn't I tell you?"

"Where did he come from?" said Mother, looking in the door.

Tootsie began barking again.

"Oh, be quiet!" said Daddy. "You'll wake the neighborhood."

"Maybe he wants a drink," said Peter.

Daddy went into the bathroom and turned on the water in the washstand. As soon as Tootsie heard the water running, she came into the bathroom. Placing her paws on the edge of the basin, she drank and drank.

In the midst of the drinking, the front door-bell rang.

"Who can that be, at this time of the morning!" said Mother.

Daddy ran and put on his bathrobe. Then he

went down to the front door. When he opened it, there stood Mr. Sawyer.

"Did I hear our dog barking?" he said.

"Well, you heard a dog all right," said Penny's daddy. "Is your dog a Great Dane?"

"She is, I regret to say," said Mr. Sawyer, stepping into the hall. "How did she get in here?"

"Hanged if I know!" said Penny's daddy. "She evidently spent the night in Penny's room."

Then he called upstairs, "Bring her down, Penny. She's Patsy's dog."

Penny brought the big dog down, while Peter and Mother hung over the banister asking questions.

"This isn't Tootsie, is it?" said Peter.

"That's Tootsie," said Mr. Sawyer, and everyone laughed.

Not long after Mr. Sawyer and Tootsie departed, Minnie arrived. She had spent the night in town. She walked into the kitchen through the back door. When she saw the empty cake plate, her jaw dropped.

"Goodness!" she cried. "Who ate all that chocolate cake?"

5

Tootsie's Second Night

Having spent her first night in Penny's chair, Tootsie seemed to think that Penny's chair was her bed. So the second night, Tootsie came and scratched on the front door of Penny's house. Penny let her in and Tootsie ran right upstairs and jumped on the big chair.

In a few moments, Patsy came after her. "Tootsie! This isn't your bed and this isn't where you live. Come home right away," said Patsy.

Patsy took hold of her collar. "Come home," she said.

Tootsie wouldn't budge, so Peter and Penny got behind Tootsie and began pushing her. It was like trying to move a rock, but finally Tootsie decided that she might as well go. She went so suddenly that Patsy sat down on the floor with a thud as Tootsie leaped over her. Peter and Penny, who were shoving from behind, fell on their faces on the chair.

Finally, Patsy got Tootsie home but she just scratched on the doors to go out again. At last, Patsy got her into her bedroom.

"You're my dog," she said, very severely, "and you must sleep in my house."

Tootsie rolled her eyes and lay down on the floor, while Patsy undressed.

In a few moments, her mother came in.

"Tootsie must learn that this is where she lives," said Patsy, "and that she must sleep where she lives."

"Yes," said Mother, "but I will be glad when Daddy builds a house for her outside. She is much too big to sleep indoors."

After Patsy was tucked into bed, Tootsie began to walk round and round the room. Patsy sat up. She patted the bed and said, "Come on, Tootsie, you can sleep in my bed."

This seemed to please Tootsie. She gave a leap and landed, with a terrific thud, on the bed. The bed shook violently. Then *Crash!*, and Patsy's bed collapsed. The spring and the mattress dropped to the floor and Patsy and Tootsie lay in a heap.

Mr. and Mrs. Sawyer heard the crash and came running to Patsy's room.

"What happened?" cried Mrs. Sawyer.

"Tootsie broke the bed," said Patsy, trying to untangle herself.

Her daddy helped her up. "My goodness!" he said. "That dog will break the house if we keep her inside much longer. I'll have to start building a kennel for her right away."

Patsy sat on a little stool and Tootsie sat in the corner watching Mr. Sawyer take off the bedcovers, lift up the mattress and then the bedspring. Finally, they were all in place again and her mother and daddy put the covers back.

Once more, Patsy was tucked into bed and Mr. and Mrs. Sawyer left her. Tootsie lay on the floor.

All was quiet and peaceful and Patsy was almost asleep when, *Ker-bang!*, the bed shook and there was Tootsie again, right on top of the

bed. Fortunately, this time, the bed didn't crash but Patsy had grabbed the covers, thinking it surely would.

"Oh, Tootsie!" she said, as Tootsie settled down. She took up so much room that Patsy was right on the edge of the bed, but soon they were both asleep.

After a while, Tootsie began to shove and she shoved and she shoved until she shoved Patsy right out of bed. Patsy picked herself up. She looked at Tootsie. She filled the center of the bed and she was sound asleep and snoring.

Patsy took her pillow and threw it on the floor. Then she pulled the blanket off the bed and wrapped herself in it. She lay down on the floor, put her head on the pillow, and went off to sleep again.

About an hour later, Tootsie woke up. She jumped to the floor and without waking Patsy, padded over to Mr. and Mrs. Sawyer's room.

She sniffed Mr. Sawyer's bed and then Mrs. Sawyer's bed. Then she went back to Mr. Sawyer and *Ker-plunk* again! She landed on Mr. Sawyer's bed.

Mr. Sawyer was dreaming that he was at the circus and when Tootsie landed on his bed, he thought an elephant had jumped on him. When he saw that it was Tootsie, he said things that should have made Tootsie realize that she wasn't welcome, but Tootsie didn't seem to mind. She wouldn't budge an inch. Mr. Sawyer was very uncomfortable but he didn't want to make any noise that would waken Patsy's mother. The bed was certainly not big enough for both Mr. Sawyer and Tootsie.

Tootsie had evidently come to stay, so Mr. Sawyer got up with a groan, pulled off a blanket, and put his pillow under his arm. He went downstairs and made his bed on the sofa in the living room. Before he fell asleep he muttered, "That dog's house is going to be built today."

Just before daybreak, Tootsie woke up again. Evidently she was a very light sleeper or else she was fussy about beds. Once more she decided to make a change.

She jumped to the floor, yawned, and stretched.

Then she gave a leap and landed with a thud on Mrs. Sawyer's bed. She woke with a start. "Oh, Tootsie!" she moaned. "Get down." But instead of getting down, Tootsie shoved herself right into the center of the bed.

"This is awful!" groaned Mrs. Sawyer. And then she rolled over and saw that Mr. Sawyer's bed was empty. She was too sleepy to wonder why it was empty. She crawled out, leaving Tootsie to enjoy her rest. She climbed into the empty bed, pulled up the comforter, and was soon asleep.

At seven o'clock, when Mrs. Sawyer went into Patsy's room to call her, she found Patsy asleep on the floor. Tootsie was asleep on the floor, too, lying close beside Patsy.

That day, a carpenter worked all day building a house for Tootsie. It was right beside the garage.

Tootsie slept that night in her own house and Patsy slept in her own bed and her daddy slept in his own bed and her mother slept in her bed. And they slept the whole night through.

6

The Cabin in the Woods

It was October now. The leaves on the trees had turned to gold and orange and bright red. One by one they fell to the ground, covering the lawns, the streets, and the sidewalks with a brilliant carpet. Peter and Penny scuffed through the leaves on their way to school. Sometimes, Penny stopped to pick up a very special leaf. He would carry it to school and put it on his teacher's desk. Penny liked to make believe that the pure gold leaves were money. "Pirates' gold pieces," he called them.

After school, the boys raked the leaves on the lawn. They swept them up into piles and when Daddy came home, he burned them. Peter and Penny loved to smell the burning leaves.

One afternoon, the boys were raking the lawn, when suddenly, the air was filled with such chirping and chattering that both of the boys looked up at the same time. The telephone and telegraph wires were filled with birds.

"Just look at the birds!" cried Penny. "Look at them! There must be a million birds."

"Yes," said Peter. "They are flying south for the winter. You wouldn't think that birds could make that much noise, would you?"

Penny laughed. He thought the birds' racket was very funny. "What do you suppose they are talking about?" he said.

Just then, Daddy appeared. "Hello, Daddy!" exclaimed Penny. "Look at all the birds."

"I have been looking at them," replied Daddy. "Sounds like a convention, doesn't it?"

"What is a 'convention,' Daddy?" asked Penny.

"A convention is a meeting of people who are all interested in the same thing. They get together to talk about it," replied Daddy.

"What do you think the birds are talking about?" asked Penny.

"Oh, they are talking about flying south. Some of them, I guess, want to go one way and some want to go another. They can't agree because they all want to stop off to see their cousins and their aunts."

Peter and Penny laughed. "I wonder who will win," said Peter.

"By the way, boys!" said Daddy. "We should have one last picnic before it gets too cold, don't you think so?"

"Oh, yes, Daddy!" cried Penny.

"A doggie roast!" cried Peter.

"Oh no! Hamburgers!" cried Penny. "Don't you want hamburgers, Daddy?"

"I'll take both," said Daddy.

"What is all this chattering about?" asked Mother, as Daddy and the boys came into the house.

"Birds," said Penny.

"Birds?" said Mother. "I thought I heard 'hamburgers.'"

Daddy and the boys laughed. "You can't hear hamburgers, Mummy," said Penny. "It's birds."

"Sillies!" laughed Mother. "I certainly heard you chattering about hamburgers."

"Oh!" cried Peter. "We thought you meant the chattering of the birds. They are all over the telephone and telegraph wires."

"Why, so they are!" exclaimed Mother, going to the window. "The fall will soon be over." Then she turned round. "Why, see here!" she cried. "We should have another picnic."

Daddy and the boys laughed. "That's just what we were saying when we came in," said Daddy.

"Hamburgers!" exclaimed Mother. "I was sure I heard you chattering about hamburgers."

"Now, you've caught up with us," laughed Daddy, putting his arm around Mother.

"Well, I'm glad of that," said Mother. "A few

more minutes and you would have been off on a picnic without me."

Daddy and the boys laughed, for they knew that a picnic without Mother is only half a picnic.

"When shall we go?" asked Peter.

"How about next Saturday?" asked Daddy.

"Swell!" said Peter and Penny in the same breath.

"Fine!" said Mother.

The next evening, when Daddy returned from the office, he said, "Mr. Ferguson, in the office, has offered us the use of his cabin up in the mountains for the weekend." And Daddy said it as though it wasn't at all important.

Peter and Penny sat up with their eyes popping. "He has!" exclaimed Peter.

"Wilikers!" cried Penny. "A cabin in the woods?"

"That's right," said Daddy. "But I don't suppose you boys want to go?"

"Want to go?" shouted Penny. "It's just what we want. A cabin in the woods."

"It sure will be a super-duper picnic," said Peter.

"We will have to take blankets," said Mother. "It will probably be very cold. But it will be wonderful."

On Friday, Daddy came home from the office early. He arrived soon after the boys came in from school.

Penny helped pile the blankets on the chair near the front door. Minnie packed a big wicker picnic basket with food for the three days. There were bread and rolls and cinnamon buns. There were bacon and eggs and frankfurters and ground meat packed in dry ice. There was a roasted chicken and a half of a baked ham. There were bottles of tomato juice, of ginger ale, and of milk. There were cans of baked beans, peas, and tomatoes. There were apples, oranges, and bananas, a pound of butter and one of Minnie's big chocolate cakes.

When Daddy looked in the basket, he shouted, "We're going to starve! Why didn't you put something in this basket, Minnie? Is this all we are going to have to live on for three days?"

"Oh, I know what cabins in the woods do to appetites," said Minnie, chuckling. "You eat three times as much. You just start cooking over a campfire and you eat and you eat till you're likely to bust."

Finally, everything was packed in the car. The two boys climbed into the back and Mother and

Daddy got in the front. They waved good-bye to Minnie and they were off.

Soon they had left the town and were out in the country. They passed cornfields with corn shocks standing in rows, and fields with large golden pumpkins waiting to be turned into pies. Sometimes the road was cut right through the woods and the leaves fell like great drops of golden rain. A pale blue smoke hung over the whole countryside and the air smelled faintly of burning leaves.

By dusk they had reached the mountains and, as the road climbed higher, the air grew colder.

"Daddy," said Penny, "do you think there are any wild animals up at the cabin?"

"Oh, there are plenty of wild animals in these mountains," replied Daddy.

"Do you think we will see any?" asked Peter.

"I can't say," replied Daddy. "Maybe if we are very quiet, we shall."

"What kind of wild animals do you think we may see?" asked Peter.

"Well, there are beavers and coon and opossums and deer," said Daddy.

"Oh, I hope I can see a deer!" cried Penny. "I would love to see a deer."

At this place the road cut through a dense wood. It was dark and Daddy put on the headlights. The light flooded the road and the dark trees rose like a wall on each side.

Suddenly, a form plunged from the darkness of the wood across the road. For a second, it was lit brilliantly by the headlights of the car. Then it was swallowed up in the darkness of the wood on the opposite side of the road. It all happened in a split second, but everyone in the car had seen that it was a beautiful deer.

The boys sat on the edge of the seat, breathless.

"Well, that was the deer you wanted to see, Penny," said Daddy.

"Wasn't it wonderful!" said Mother, in a whisper.

"Yes," replied Penny, "but I wanted to see it longer. Oh, I would love to see one longer."

"Well, perhaps we will see one tomorrow," said Daddy.

At last they turned into a narrow road that was like a ribbon of light through the woods.

"Are we almost there, Daddy?" asked Peter. "I'm awfully hungry."

"Almost," replied Daddy.

Finally, the car came to a stop in what seemed to Peter and Penny to be the middle of the woods.

Now that the motor of the car was silent, they could hear the gentle *lap, lap* of the water.

"I hear water, Daddy," said Penny.

"That's the lake," replied Daddy.

"Oh, Daddy! I didn't know there was a lake," said Penny.

"Yes, indeed," said Daddy. "The cabin is very near the lake."

Daddy took the flashlight out of the pocket of the car. "You stay in the car," he said, "until I put the lights on in the cabin."

Mother, Peter, and Penny watched Daddy follow the path of the flashlight. Now he was going up some steps. Now he was on a porch. He must be putting the key in the door. Now he was inside.

Then, suddenly, bright lights twinkled in the darkness. They were the lighted windows of the cabin. Penny had been feeling cold but now he felt warm right down into his little toes.

This was like a dream come true. This was the cabin in the woods.

7

It's a Wolf

Peter and Penny were delighted when they saw the inside of the cabin. There was a big open fireplace where they soon had a fire burning.

They were as hungry as bears and gobbled up the chicken sandwiches and hot cocoa that Mother fixed for their supper. But they didn't tarry long, they were so anxious to get into the bunk beds. They spent quite some time, however, climbing up and down the ladder that led to the upper bunk. Daddy said that they were like monkeys on a stick.

Both of the boys wanted to sleep in the upper bunk, so it was finally settled that Peter would sleep in it on Friday night and Penny would sleep in it on Saturday night.

This satisfied both Penny and Peter and before long they were tucked away and sound asleep.

In the middle of the night, Penny woke up. He wondered where he was. He sat up in bed

and looked around. Everything looked so strange and there was a woody odor. It smelled a little like being in the cedar closet at home.

Penny got up and went to the window. When he looked out of the window, things looked even more strange. A mist lay over everything and moonlight filtered through the mist. Penny felt certain that something was about to happen. Sure enough, in a moment, a beautiful stag appeared between the trees. The moonlight shone on his back and his antlers as he moved silently toward the water. Penny held his breath. Then, in a moment, he saw another deer. This one, he knew, was the doe, for she had no antlers. He watched as she followed the stag to the edge of the water. There they both bent their heads and drank. Then, as quietly as they had come, they disappeared.

Penny let out his breath and turned away from the window. Suddenly, he knew where he was. He was in the cabin in the mountains and that big lump in the bunk up near the ceiling was Peter.

In the morning, he told Peter and Mother and Daddy about the deer he had seen. "It was just like being in a fairy story," said Penny.

"Why didn't you call us?" asked Peter.

"I don't know," said Penny. "I guess I forgot you were here. And I was afraid if I moved, it would all disappear."

When breakfast was over, Peter and Penny went down to the lake. It was too cold to go swimming so they took the rowboat out of the boathouse and rowed out to a little island in the lake. From here they could see a few other cabins, dotted around the edge of the lake. Far away, they heard a dog barking.

The boys explored the little island and then rowed back to the mainland.

At lunch, Peter said, "Daddy, is it all right if we take a walk around the edge of the lake?"

"Certainly," said Daddy, "but don't get so far into the woods that you lose sight of the lake. As long as you keep the lake in view you will know how to come home."

"Okay," said Peter.

"Do you think we will meet any wild animals?" asked Penny.

"Well, keep your eyes open," replied Daddy.

"I would like to explore a stream and find a beaver's dam, wouldn't you, Penny?" said Peter.

"Oh yes!" cried Penny. "What do you think, Daddy? Do you think we could?"

"Suppose we explore a stream tomorrow?" said Daddy.

"All right," said the boys, as they trotted down the path to the lake. Near the edge of the lake, they turned off on a path that led around the lake. They scuffed their feet through the red and yellow leaves. They picked up nuts and

pinecones. They heard the crackle of twigs under their feet and the rustle of squirrels in the branches overhead. They were pretty far from home now. They were alone in what seemed to be a very big forest. And then, all of a sudden, they heard a sound. It was a low growl. Peter and Penny looked around. There was another growl.

"What's that?" Penny whispered.

About a foot away, Peter saw an animal. Its eyes shone like big bright marbles. It was a brindle gray color. Its pointed ears stood up and its long plumelike tail switched back and forth.

"It's a wolf!" cried Peter. "Run, Penny!"

The two boys started off as fast as their legs could carry them. The wolf bounded after them.

"Climb a tree!" cried Peter.

Penny ran to the nearest pine tree. The branches were low enough for him to get a foothold. Then up he scrambled. Peter did the same. When they looked for each other, they were in two trees about ten feet apart. Penny was trembling so hard he shook the branches. He looked down for the wolf. There he was, smelling around the base of the trees.

"What shall we do?" said Penny.

"I have a whistle in my pocket," said Peter. "I'll blow it and maybe Daddy will hear it and come."

"But I don't want the wolf to attack Daddy," said Penny.

"Oh no," said Peter. "If Daddy could just bring a gun and shoot it. But if I blow the whistle, he won't know that he is to bring a gun. I guess I had better not blow it."

The wolf sat down and looked up in the trees.

"He has a very vicious face," said Penny. "His eyes are just like fire."

"Now he's licking his chops," said Peter. "And look at his terrible teeth."

"Oh, dear!" cried Penny. "Maybe we'll have to stay here all night." And Penny began to cry.

"Now, don't cry, Penny," said Peter. "Daddy will come to find us."

"But I don't want Daddy to get eaten by a wolf," Penny wailed.

Just then the wolf lifted his head and howled. He howled and he howled.

"Oh, dear!" cried Penny. "He wants to eat us, doesn't he?"

"Maybe Daddy will hear that and bring a gun," said Peter.

"Oh, I hope so," said Penny. "He's a very vicious wolf, isn't he?"

"He sure is," said Peter. "But he can't get up the trees."

The wolf, at this point, quieted. He decided to

lie on the ground. He put his head down between his front feet. The boys looked down upon him from the trees.

"Maybe he is going to sleep," said Penny.

Peter said nothing. He just continued to stare down at the animal.

After some little time, he said, "Penny, do you see something shining on the back of the wolf's neck?"

Penny looked down. "Uh-huh!" he said.

"What do you suppose it is?" said Peter.

"I don't know. I guess it's just his fur," replied Penny.

Peter moved down to a lower limb. He looked as closely as he could. Then he said, "Penny, it's a collar. It's a dog collar."

"What's a wolf doing with a dog collar?" asked Penny.

"Maybe he isn't a wolf," said Peter. "I guess maybe he's a dog."

"Do you think so?" asked Penny.

Peter climbed to a still lower limb. Then he said, "Here, boy. Come here."

The animal got up and walked over to the foot of the tree. He wagged his tail and said, "Woof!"

Peter got down to the ground. He held out his fist and the dog sniffed it. Then Peter patted him on the head. "Nice doggie!" he said. The dog rubbed against him.

"Come on down, Penny," Peter called. "It's only a dog."

Penny came down and he, too, patted the dog.

Just then, a man appeared coming toward them through the woods. The dog galloped off to meet him, barking happy barks.

"So you've been making new friends, Toastie!" he said.

"Is he your dog, sir?" asked Peter.

"Yes," replied the gentleman. "He looks pretty fierce, doesn't he? But he's just as gentle as a lamb. We call him 'Toastie.'" Then he chuckled. "Short for 'Milk Toast,'" he said. "Some people think he's a wolf. Looks like one, doesn't he?"

"Well," said Peter, "he does, a little."

"But I think almost anybody would know he is a dog," said Penny. "Don't you?"

8

Exploring the Stream

The next morning, Peter and Penny and Daddy set out to explore a stream. Mother packed their lunch basket. There were frankfurters that they were going to cook over an open fire. Peter wore the frying pan dangling from a strap that he wore over his shoulder.

On the opposite side of the lake was the mouth of a stream. Daddy said he thought that would be a good stream to explore. So they climbed into the rowboat and rowed across. When they landed, Daddy secured the boat by tying it to an old tree stump.

The three explorers walked along the bank of the stream. It was about twelve feet wide and the water was as clear as crystal. The pebbles and stones on the bottom looked as though they had been scrubbed, they were so clean. Here and there were big rocks and whenever it was possible the boys crossed the stream by stepping from rock to rock.

"One of you fellows will drop the lunch in the stream, if you don't watch out," said Daddy. "You had better let me carry the basket."

Peter handed over the basket to Daddy. The three swung along, whistling.

Sometimes the trees and bushes grew so close to the stream that one could hardly find a foothold, but they pressed on because it was all new and exciting.

Finally they came to a place where the bank was very high above the stream. Here they had to walk carefully. Daddy lifted a heavy branch so that Peter and Penny could pass under it. As he lifted it, the basket on his arm tilted and the package of frankfurters flew out of the basket, the paper opened, and they fell in a shower down to the stream.

"Oh, Daddy!" cried Peter and Penny together. "The hot dogs!"

The three looked down as the frankfurters dove into the water. They watched them float downstream—one, two, three, four, five, six, seven, eight, nine of them—all pink and plump.

"Well!" exclaimed Daddy. "Guess they'll be cold dogs forever now."

"Oh, Daddy!" cried Penny. "Now we'll have to eat the rolls with nothing in them but mustard."

"Isn't that the limit!" said Daddy. "I am so sorry."

Peter and Penny looked very gloomy indeed as they continued on their way. Before very long, they were close to the stream again and there were stepping-stones so that they could cross the stream. When they reached the middle of the stream, Penny said, "Look, Daddy. What makes those little splashes in the water and the ripples?"

Daddy looked where Penny was pointing. "Oh!" exclaimed Daddy. "That must be a school of trout."

The ripples came nearer and under the surface of the water, there appeared to be a dark shadow. As it came closer, Penny could see that what looked like a shadow was a school of fish.

To the surprise of the boys, as the fish passed Daddy quickly reached into the water and when he pulled out his hand he had a trout in it.

"Quick, Peter!" he said. "Take the rolls out of the basket."

Peter took the rolls out of the basket and Daddy put the fish in. He put a rock on top of it to keep it from jumping out. Then he looked down in the water again. In a moment, he had another trout. He popped it into the basket and put in another stone.

Peter's and Penny's eyes were as round as saucers. "Oh, Daddy!" said Penny. "Do you think you can catch another one?"

"I'll try," replied Daddy.

They waited, holding their breath. Soon Daddy plunged his arm into the stream again and once more, he pulled up a fish. "That water is just like ice," he said.

"How did you ever learn to catch fish that way, Daddy?" asked Peter.

"It's an old trick someone taught me when I was a boy."

"It's some trick!" said Penny.

"Well, now we have our lunch, haven't we, Daddy?" said Peter.

"You bet we have," replied Daddy. "A much better lunch than we lost."

"Isn't it time to eat?" asked Penny. "I'm hungry."

"Well, let's get started, anyway," said Daddy. "It will take us a little while to build the fire and get going."

The boys started to gather sticks for the fire and Daddy set to work to clean the fish. He opened them up with his knife and washed them in the stream.

When the boys had gathered enough sticks, they built the fire. Before very long, it was burning well. When there were enough red embers, Daddy put some butter in the frying pan. When it was sizzling, he laid the three fish in the pan.

"Oh! Wilikers!" cried Penny. "Isn't this exciting?"

"Real surprise party, isn't it?" said Daddy.

"Smells wonderful," said Peter.

Then suddenly, Penny cried out, "We haven't any forks. How are we going to eat the fish?"

Peter and Daddy laughed. "Penny certainly is civilized, isn't he, Daddy?" said Peter.

"He certainly is," replied Daddy. "I guess he wants fish knives and forks with pearl handles."

They all laughed and Daddy lifted the golden brown fish from the pan and placed each one on a paper plate. At first, they were too hot to touch but they soon cooled. Peter, Penny, and Daddy ate a delicious lunch and they didn't put mustard on their rolls.

When they had finished, Peter held up his ten fingers and said, "What! No finger bowls!"

And Daddy called out, "Minnie! The cut-glass finger bowls, please."

The boys laughed.

Then Daddy said, "'Smatter with Minnie?"

"Fell in the stream, I guess," said Peter.

"In that case, I guess we'll have to wash in the stream," said Daddy.

They all went, laughing, to the stream.

Afterward, they made certain that the fire was out. Then they packed the soiled dishes into the basket and started off again. "I think we had better be getting back to Mother," said Daddy.

"But we haven't found any beaver dams," said Penny.

"No," said Daddy, "but perhaps the beavers haven't been building dams lately. Maybe we can come again and next time we will find one."

"Oh, Daddy, do you think we can come again?" asked Peter and Penny in one breath.

"Maybe so," said Daddy.

They retraced their steps, crossing and re-crossing the stream, until they reached a bend in it. As they rounded the bend, there came into view a log that lay partly across the stream. There, snuggled against the log, were—one, two, three, four, five, six, seven, eight, nine hot dogs. They looked very forlorn and out of place.

Daddy saw them first and he threw back his head and laughed a great big laugh. When he

pointed them out to the boys, they all laughed very hard.

They walked out on the log and looked at the plump, pink weenies. "Let's take them home," cried Penny. "They're just as good as new. The water is so clean and cold. Don't you think it is all right to take them home, Daddy?"

"Sure!" said Daddy. "Gather them up."

The boys picked them all up and wrapped them in some paper napkins that were in the basket.

When they reached the mouth of the stream, they were all pretty tired. The little boys were glad to get into the rowboat and have Daddy row them across the lake. They ran up from the landing and into the cabin, shouting, "Oh, Mother! What do you think? We brought the hot dogs back."

9

Peter the Worker

Peter and Penny returned from their weekend wanting more than anything else in the
world a cabin in the mountains.

First one and then the other would say,
"Can't we have a cabin like Mr. Ferguson's?"

"I don't know about that," Daddy would
reply.

"It would be fun," Penny would say. "We

would surely find a beaver's dam if we owned a cabin and could go often."

"And it would be wonderful in the wintertime," said Peter. "We could skate on the lake and we could ski."

"Now, Peter, what do you know about skating and skiing?" asked Mother.

"Nothing," replied Peter, "but I could learn. I have seen them skate and ski in the movies. It looks like a lot of fun."

The boys spoke of the cabin very often and each time Daddy would say, "Well, I don't know."

One evening the telephone rang. Peter ran to answer it. "Daddy," he called, "Mr. Ferguson wants to speak to you." Daddy picked up the telephone. He listened for a long time to what Mr. Ferguson had to say. Then he replied, "Well, I don't know what to do about it. If I had some extra money I would be all right."

Peter got up. As he left the room, he thought Daddy looked worried. When Peter reached his own room he didn't go on reading his book. Instead, he sat on the window seat thinking. He wondered what Daddy needed money for. Daddy had always seemed to have money. He just reached into his pocket and there was always some there. Peter began to wonder whether it cost Daddy very much to have two boys. After all, he had only had Penny and now he had two boys, so that must cost twice as much.

Peter didn't want his daddy to be worried about his money, so he said to himself, "I know what I will do! I'll get another paper route. I made out very well when I lived in the home."

Peter decided that he wouldn't say anything about his paper route. He would just go out after school and see if he could get some customers.

The next afternoon, Peter started out right after school. He didn't go back to the neighborhood where he used to serve papers. Bob Williams had taken over that route and Peter didn't want to take Bob's customers away from him. So Peter went from house to house. He tried several sections of the town but everyone seemed to have a paperboy. He came home feeling a little discouraged.

Peter hoped that Daddy wasn't having too much trouble about his money. He remembered a movie that he had seen where a little boy's father had lost all of his money and he had to give up the house they lived in. Peter did hope that Daddy wouldn't have to sell the house they lived in. It was such a nice house.

The next day, Peter tried again to get some customers for papers. But everyone seemed to have a paperboy. He decided that he would have to try something else.

He stopped in the drugstore to see if the druggist needed a boy to run errands. The druggist said, "No." He had a boy. But he took Peter's name and address and telephone number. He said he would get in touch with Peter if he needed a boy.

Peter stopped at three grocery stores. He received the same news at each. They all took his name and address and telephone number. Then he stopped at the livery stable to see if they needed a boy. They said, "No. We have a boy."

That night he was very much discouraged. He didn't seem able to earn a penny.

The next morning, when he woke up, the ground was covered with a heavy fall of snow. It had snowed all night and, best of all, it was Saturday. Now Peter saw a chance to make some money. He would shovel pavements.

It was still very early, but Peter scrambled into his clothes and went down to the kitchen. No one was down yet, so he ate a bowl of cereal and a cin-namon bun and drank a glass of chocolate milk. Then he put on his snowsuit and rubber boots. He left a note on the kitchen table. This is what it said: Gone to shovel pavements—Peter.

Peter took the snow shovel and the broom out of the garage. He flung them up to his shoulder and started out. The snow was very deep and he made fresh tracks out to the sidewalk and up the street.

A few doors away, he saw a neighbor, Mrs. Cooper, taking the milk in off the front step.

"Hello, Mrs. Cooper!" Peter called. "Want your pavement cleaned?"

"How much do you charge?" said Mrs. Cooper.

"I don't know," Peter replied. "I'll do it for whatever you want to pay me."

"All right," said Mrs. Cooper. "Go ahead."

Peter set to work and he did a good job. When he finished, the pavement was clean. He rang Mrs. Cooper's doorbell and when she came to the door, she said, "That's a fine job, Peter. Come inside and have a cup of hot cocoa and I'll pay you."

Peter followed Mrs. Cooper into the kitchen. He drank the cocoa and ate a piece of toast.

Then Mrs. Cooper gave him a quarter. Peter thanked her and set out again.

More people were awake now, so he rang the doorbells. Each one asked, "How much?" And to each one he replied, "Whatever you want to pay me." So everyone said, "Sure. You can shovel the snow off the pavement."

By lunchtime, Peter had earned a dollar and a half and he felt quite rich.

When he sat down to eat his lunch his cheeks looked like red apples.

"Peter," said Minnie, "Mr. Jones, the grocery man, telephoned. He wants to know if you can deliver orders this afternoon. His boy's out."

"Oh, sure!" said Peter.

"And the drugstore man, he telephoned and he wants to know if you will stop by and deliver some orders for him about five o'clock."

"Sure!" said Peter. "Gee! This is great."

"And the livery stable man, he telephoned."

Peter's eyes were just about ready to pop out of his head.

"The livery stable man?" said Peter.

"Yes," said Minnie. "He wants to know if you can sweep up for him about six o'clock."

"Sweep up for him?" Peter repeated. "About six o'clock? Oh, sure! Sure!"

"Well," said Minnie, "if you're going to be such a business man, I just wish you'd get yourself a secretary to answer the telephone, because I've got my work to do."

Peter laughed. "I'm making money, Minnie," he said.

"Well, I hope you can afford a secretary pretty soon," said Minnie.

As soon as Peter finished his lunch, he ran over to the grocer's. He went out with the man who drove the truck and helped him deliver the orders.

At five o'clock, he was at the drugstore. He delivered all that the druggist gave him.

At six o'clock, he rushed into the livery stable. "Here you are," the manager of the stables called out. "Here's the broom. Sweep everything up to this trapdoor. Then drop it into the manure pit."

Peter set to work. He swept the floor carefully. When everything was swept up to the trapdoor, he opened it and began to sweep the pile down into the bin below. It was all down and Peter was giving one extra swish with the broom, when he slipped and went *Zoop!* right down into the manure pit.

The stable man came running. He looked

down into the pit. There was Peter just picking himself up.

"Are you all right?" the man called. "Here, give me your hands and I'll pull you out."

Peter held up his hands and the man pulled him out. "Are you all right?" he repeated.

"Yes," said Peter. "But I was awful surprised."

"And you're an awful mess," said the man, as he reached for a whisk broom and began to brush Peter off.

When he was finally clean, the man paid Peter twenty cents and Peter set off for home and his dinner. He was a tired but happy boy. He had made three dollars since he woke up that morning.

When he went into the house, his mother said, "Why, Peter! Darling! We thought you were never coming home."

"I've been working, Mummy," said Peter.

Then his mother wrinkled up her nose. She looked puzzled. Then she said, "Darling! What is that terrible smell?"

"Oh, I guess that's me," replied Peter. "I fell into the manure pit."

"Oh, Peter!" she cried. "You didn't hurt yourself, did you?"

"No, I'm okay," replied Peter.

"Well, go take a bath, dear," said Mother. "And don't work at the livery stable again, please."

"But I got twenty cents, Mother," said Peter.

"Well, dear one, I'll pay you twenty cents if you will promise never to smell like that again."

Peter laughed as he climbed the stairs to take his bath.

When he was all clean again, he suddenly felt as though his legs just wouldn't hold him up any longer. He was so glad when Mother said, "Now, how about tucking into bed and I'll bring your supper on a tray?"

It sounded too wonderful to Peter. The change from the manure pit to supper in bed was about like changing from a frog into a prince.

"Oh, Mummy! That would be wonderful!" he cried, flinging his arms around her.

When he had finished his supper, he snuggled down into his soft bed. Just as he was dozing off to sleep, he heard the telephone bell ring. In a few moments, Mother came to his bed.

"Peter," she said, "Bob Williams is on the telephone. He wants to know if you would like to have your paper route back."

Peter opened one eye. "Oh, sure! Sure!" he said.

And before his mother got back to the telephone, Peter was sound asleep.

10

Now It Is Christmas

Peter took over his paper route and all of his customers were glad to see him again. It seemed like old times to meet the newspaper truck and to trundle his express wagon. Very often, Penny went with Peter and helped him deliver his papers. At the end of the week, when Peter collected his money, he put all of it in his bank.

The first week, he offered to give part of it to Penny but when Penny heard that Peter was working to help Daddy, Penny said, "No, I want to help Daddy, too. You put it all in the bank."

When Peter had saved up five dollars, he felt very rich. He was so happy when he went to Daddy with it. It had all been in small change, but now he had a five-dollar bill.

"Daddy," he said, holding out the five-dollar bill, "I have five dollars for you."

"For me!" exclaimed Daddy.

"Yes," replied Peter. "I earned it."

"Well, Peter! That is fine but you keep it, son. It's yours," said Daddy.

"Oh, but I earned it for you, Daddy!" said Peter. "I earned it on purpose for you. I heard you say that you needed some money."

"Why, Peter! Dear boy!" said Daddy. "That was wonderful of you. But I wouldn't think of taking your money. You use it to buy Christmas presents."

"Oh, no, Daddy! I heard you say that you wished you had some money," said Peter. "And I want very much to give it to you."

Daddy put his arm around Peter and said, "Peter, I am going to tell you why I said that. I wanted to buy something that I knew we all would enjoy. I didn't think I could afford it, but now I have almost all of the money to pay for it."

"Oh, Daddy! What is it?" said Peter.

"Well, I am keeping it a secret from Mother," said Daddy, "because I thought it would be nice to have it a Christmas surprise. But I'll tell you, if you think you can keep it a secret."

"Oh, yes, Daddy!" said Peter.

Daddy leaned over and whispered the secret in Peter's ear. Peter looked very much surprised and very delighted. "Oh, Daddy!" he cried. "How wonderful! How much more money do you need?"

"Well," said Daddy, "just about five dollars."

"Oh, isn't that wonderful!" said Peter. "Here's my five dollars. Now you can buy it."

"That's just great, Peter," said Daddy. "Now it will be from both of us to Mother."

"From Penny, too," said Peter, "because he didn't take anything for helping me deliver papers."

"All right. That's fine," said Daddy, as he reached into his vest pocket.

Peter watched Daddy put the five-dollar bill

in his wallet. He felt very proud, giving Daddy five dollars that he had earned.

Daddy put the wallet in his pocket and said, "Peter, I can't tell you how much this five dollars means to me. To think that you went out and earned it for me. I'm proud to have you for my son."

Just then, Mother called from upstairs. "Peter!" she called. "It is time for you to go to bed."

"I'm coming, Mother," Peter replied. "Good night, Daddy."

Peter kissed his daddy good night and Daddy pulled out his wallet again.

"Peter," he said, "here is some money with which to buy your Christmas presents."

Daddy gave Peter five one-dollar bills.

"But, Daddy!" said Peter. "Aren't you giving back to me the five dollars that I gave you?"

"Not at all! This is the five dollars you gave me," said Daddy, patting the five-dollar bill. "And, Peter, my boy, it means a great deal to me. More than I can ever tell you."

"Well, thanks, Daddy, for the Christmas money," said Peter, as he stuffed the five one-dollar bills into his pocket. "Good night."

"Good night, Peter," said Daddy.

About two weeks before Christmas, Daddy said, "Mr. Ferguson says we can spend Christmas in his cabin."

"Oh, Daddy!" cried Peter and Penny in one breath. "That's wonderful!" And Peter's eyes twinkled when he looked at Daddy.

"Would you like it, Mother?" asked Daddy.

"I would like nothing better," replied Mother. "You know how I love the cabin."

"How long can we stay?" asked Penny.

"Just over the weekend," replied Daddy.

"Where will we have our Christmas tree?" asked Penny.

"I think it would be best to have it here," said Daddy. "We can trim it before we go and it will be here when we get back."

"Oh, Daddy!" cried Penny. "Couldn't Peter and I trim the tree ourselves this year?"

"What do you think of that, Mother?" asked Daddy.

"I don't see any reason why not," said Mother.

"Oh, goodie!" cried Penny. "Shall we let Patsy help?"

"Sure," said Peter.

A few days before Christmas, Peter, Penny,

and Daddy went out and bought a Christmas tree. Daddy put it in the living-room alcove where it would be out of the way. It was a bushy tree but it only reached halfway to the ceiling. Daddy said that was big enough because they were going to trim it themselves.

Two days before Christmas, the boys carried the boxes of Christmas tree balls downstairs from the attic.

Penny telephoned to Patsy and Patsy came over to help trim the tree. Tootsie came with her. By this time, Tootsie was just like Mary's little lamb. She followed Patsy wherever she went.

"Hello, Patsy!" the two boys called out when Patsy came into the house.

"Hello!" replied Patsy, walking into the living room. "Isn't it exciting to trim the Christmas tree? Daddy and Mother won't let me help with our Christmas tree. But they said maybe I could next year. Anyway, I'm going to help trim yours now."

The boys patted Tootsie and then she settled her great self down before the open fire.

"Well, now!" said Penny. "Here are the boxes of balls and here are the tree hooks and here are the packages of silver. Look, it looks just like spiderwebs when you put it on the tree."

"Hey!" cried Peter. "Don't put it on now, Penny. It goes on last. After all the balls are on."

"I know. I was just showing Patsy," said Penny.

"Now, be careful of those balls, Patsy," said Peter. "Don't break any."

"All right," replied Patsy, as she lifted a box off the top of the pile and put it on the seat of a nearby chair. "I'll be careful."

Penny lifted the lid of a box and uncovered twelve beautiful red balls. He put a hook through the little tin loop on each ball and hung them on the tree. At the same time, Peter was hanging striped balls.

The balls that Patsy was hanging were silver. When she looked at them, she could see her own face. Only it was a funny Patsy face. The side of the ball made her face look very broad and her cheeks stuck out on each side like a chipmunk with nuts in its cheeks. Patsy got the giggles.

"Stop giggling, Patsy," said Penny. "You'll break a ball if you're not careful."

"I'm being careful," said Patsy.

Peter's next box of balls looked like brightly

painted tops, while Penny's were red bells. They tinkled when he shook them.

Patsy finished hanging her silver balls and picked up the next box. When she lifted the lid, there were twelve golden reindeer.

"Be very careful of those reindeer," said Penny. "They're very special."

"I am careful," said Patsy, as she hung a reindeer on a branch of the Christmas tree.

"Say! It's beginning to look nice!" said Penny. And he flopped himself down on the nearest chair. Immediately, there was the crunching sound of breaking Christmas tree balls. Penny's eyebrows flew up in surprise as he lifted himself out of the chair. There, on the seat of the chair, was a broken box and six crushed balls.

"Oh, Penny!" cried Patsy and Peter together. "Look what you did!"

"I didn't see the box on the chair," said Penny.

"Well, you should have looked," said Peter. "That was the box I was using. Now look at them! Just look at them! Nothing but crumbles."

"I'm sorry," said Penny.

"Well, you have to be more careful," said Peter. "Look out there, Patsy! You nearly dropped an angel."

Penny gathered up the crumpled cardboard box and the crumbled glass and threw all of it into the fireplace.

The tree was beginning to look very lovely but there was still a long way to go before it would be finished. Peter stood off and admired it. "It's going to look awfully pretty," he said.

Penny picked up another box of balls. He removed the lid and began to hang golden stars on the tree.

"I'm thirsty," said Peter. "I'm going to get a glass of milk."

"So am I," said Penny. "Come on, Patsy, let's get a glass of milk."

The three children traipsed out to the kitchen. Minnie poured out three glasses of milk and the children returned to the living room. They each carried a glass of milk in one hand and a cookie in the other.

"Now, don't sit on any balls," said Peter.

They all sat down without sitting on any balls. They sat munching their cookies and drinking their milk and admiring the Christmas tree.

"I'm going to get another cookie," said Peter, putting his glass on a small table.

"Bring me another, too," said Penny. "And one for Patsy."

"Okay!" replied Peter, as he left the room.

Tootsie, who had been asleep in front of the fireplace, got up and followed Peter to the door of the living room. There, just inside of the door, she lay down.

In a few moments, Peter came back with the cookies. As he passed Tootsie, he tripped over her big paw. Peter didn't fall but he kept right on tripping and he tripped all the way through the living room and headed right for the alcove and the Christmas tree.

Penny and Patsy sat watching this performance in amazement. It didn't seem possible that Peter was going to crash into the Christmas tree. But he went right on tripping, straight into the alcove. And then, *Crash!*, down came the tree, balls, Peter, cookies, and all.

The children were so surprised that they were speechless. Peter lay on the floor, not knowing exactly what had happened.

Just then, Daddy appeared in the doorway.

"Great snakes!" he cried. "What is going on?"

When he saw Peter lying under the Christmas

tree, he couldn't help laughing. This made Patsy and Penny laugh, too.

"I don't think it is funny," muttered Peter from under the tree. And then Peter did something that he hardly ever did. He began to cry.

"Oh, come!" said Daddy, picking up the tree. "You're not hurt, are you?"

"No," said Peter, "but I made such an awful mess of the Christmas tree. Look at all of the balls I broke."

Daddy stood the tree upright. By a miracle, there were still a lot of balls that had not broken.

Peter brought the dustpan and brush and swept up the broken balls. Every once in a while he had to wipe away a tear.

The children finished the tree by dinnertime. Not once did anyone say, "Be careful. Don't drop the Christmas tree balls."

The following day, Daddy and Mother, Peter and Penny left for the cabin. Peter sat in the back of the car in the midst of packages of all sizes and shapes. There were also boxes and the big picnic basket, bulging with everything for Christmas dinner.

The ride up into the mountains was very different from the last time. Now, in place of the yellow, orange, pink, and red of the leaves, the bare branches of the trees showed gray against the paler gray sky. They passed brown fields with patches of snow, left over from the last snowstorm. The only bright color was the green of the fields sown with winter wheat.

"That sky looks full of snow," said Daddy. "We'll probably have snow before morning."

"Oh, goodie!" cried Penny.

"I hope so!" said Peter.

Sure enough, by the time they reached the cabin, it was snowing very hard.

"Oh, I hope I am going to get those skis I asked for," said Peter, looking at a very long package that stuck way up inside of the car.

"No fair guessing," said Daddy. "You are supposed to be looking out of the window, Peter."

Peter laughed. "All right," he said.

When they drove up to the cabin, the roof and the steps and the pine trees looked as though they had been dusted freely with powdered sugar. The snow was falling so hard that it hid the lake from view.

"Now, you wait here a few minutes," said Daddy, "while I unlock the door and light the fire."

Daddy got out of the car and took some bags out of the back. He carried them up the steps and went into the cabin. In a few minutes, smoke was curling out of the chimney.

When Daddy returned to the car, he said, "Come on, now. The fire is burning."

Peter, Penny, and Mother got out of the car. With their arms filled with bundles and boxes, they paraded up the path to the cabin. When they reached the door, there, hanging on the doorknob, was a great big Christmas card. It said, "Love and a Merry Christmas to Mother, from Daddy and the boys."

Mother was so surprised she hardly knew what to say.

"Sorry we couldn't wrap it up in cellophane
and tie it with red ribbon," said Daddy.

Mother laughed. "It's wonderful !" she cried.
"Just wonderful!" Then she kissed Daddy and
Penny and Peter. "Thank you so much," she
said.

Inside, the cabin looked very cheery, with the
fire roaring in the fireplace.

It took a long time to unload the car and
stow everything away in the cabin. When they
had finished Daddy said, "Well, boys! What do

you say we go out and trim another Christmas tree?"

"What do you mean?" cried Penny.

"I thought it would be nice to trim one for the birds," said Daddy.

"Oh, Daddy!" cried Peter. "That would be great! What will we use for trimmings?"

"Oh, I have brought the trimmings," said Daddy, picking up a box.

The boys followed Daddy outside. They picked out a small pine tree near the steps.

Soon they were all at work trimming the tree. They hung the branches with pieces of suet and cranberries and little metal cups filled with different kinds of seeds. Daddy also had some tiny red apples that they hung here and there. Near the top, they hung a loaf of bread.

In the midst of the trimming, Daddy said with a laugh, "Careful now, Peter, don't drop any balls."

Peter laughed. "Well, anyway," he said, "this is one Christmas tree I can't knock over, even if I try."

Turn the page for a peek at another
Carolyn Haywood classic

Primrose Day

where there's always a reason to be merry!

1

Merry Leaves for America

Merry Primrose Ramsay was almost seven years old. She was named Merry because her mother loved merry little girls and Primrose because she was born in the month of April when the primroses bloom in England.

Merry lived in England in the big city of London. When asked whom she lived with, she would reply, "I live with my mummy and daddy, Greggie and Molly and Annie." Greggie was a Scottie dog whose name was really Mac-Gregor. Molly was a make-believe playmate and Annie was the cook.

When people asked Merry where she lived she would say, "I live at number eight Heartford Square." Then everyone knew that Merry lived in a house that faced a little park. Merry was glad she lived in a house on a square. She liked walking past the houses on one side of the square, then across the end of the square and down the other side. The houses were built of red brick and they all had white stone steps. They were very close together. Merry thought they looked like faces with their cheeks touching. The square was a cozy place to live.

But the nicest part about living on the square was the little park. All around the park there was a high iron railing. There was a gate at each end. The people who lived on the square had keys so that they could go in and out of the gates. There were flower beds and trees in the park. In the spring there were tulips in the flower beds. The paths were covered with pebbles and sometimes Merry would find a very pretty pebble. Then she would put it in her pocket and carry it home to show to Mummy.

There were benches in the park, too. On clear days there were always nurses sitting on the benches. They watched over the little children while they played. All of the nurses were called "Nanny." Merry had had a nanny when she was little but now that she was almost seven years old, she didn't need a nurse to watch her. She was old enough to take care of herself.

One afternoon Merry stood at the front window. It was February and it was raining. No one was in the park. The benches were shiny wet. The bare trees dripped. Tiny rivers ran between the pebbles in the paths. Merry pressed her nose against the windowpane. "Do you know what, Molly?" she said to her make-believe playmate.

"I'm going to America. I'm going to America to stay with Aunt Helen and Uncle Bill and my cousin Jerry. You see, Molly, it's because of the war. Mummy says when people are selfish and afraid of each other they go to war and hurt each other. All of the boys and girls in my school have gone away from London. Mummy and Daddy are sending me to America until the war is all over. I'm going all by myself, too. Daddy can't go because he is doing very important work for the King. And Mummy can't go because England needs her, too. So I'm going alone."

Merry turned away from the window and began to set out her doll's tea set. When Greggie heard the rattle of the dishes, he came into the room. Greggie knew that where there are dishes there may be food. He never missed any if he could help it.

"Greggie, you are going to America, too," said Merry.

Greggie cocked one ear.

"And I'm going to take you, too, Molly. Do you think you will like to go to America?"

Just then the front door closed. Merry set a cup on the table and ran to the head of the stairs. Greggie tore along at her heels.

"Daddy!" she called. "Is that you, Daddy?"

"Right you are!" called Daddy.

Merry started down the stairs at a run. Halfway down, she stopped still. Daddy stood at the bottom of the stairs. He was wearing a soldier's uniform. Merry hadn't seen her daddy in a soldier's uniform before. He looked strange and different. Merry went down the last six steps very slowly. Her face was grave and her eyes were very big. When she reached the second step, Daddy took her in his arms. "How do you like me, little one?" he asked.

"All right," murmured Merry, "only you don't look like Daddy."

Daddy rubbed his cheek against Merry's. "Do I feel like Daddy?" he asked.

Merry hugged him very tight. "Yes," she said, "you scratch like Daddy." Then they both laughed.

The night before Merry was to leave for America, her mummy packed her bag. She put in all of Merry's winter clothes and all of her summer clothes, her underwear, and her stockings. She packed her winter pajamas and her summer nightgowns. On the very top she placed her warm dressing gown. Her shoes and her bedroom slippers were tucked in the side of the suitcase. Into a little rubber envelope, she put Merry's toothbrush and sponge. Merry sat on the bed and watched her. At last the lid was closed. Merry heard the lock snap shut.

"Mummy," said Merry, "do you think you could sleep in my bed tonight?"

"Yes, darling," said Mummy. "I'll sleep in your bed tonight."

Merry lay in her bed and waited for Mummy. She wondered why it took Mummy so long to get ready for bed. At last she came. She turned out the light beside the bed. Then she lay down beside her little girl. "Oh, Mummy!" cried Merry, "you have lain right on top of Molly!"

"Dear, dear!" said Mummy. "It is so hard for me to know where Molly is. Do you think she will mind very much?"

"Well, if you could lift up a little, she could get out," said Merry.

Mummy lifted up a little. "Now I hope Molly has found a comfortable spot," she said.

Merry snuggled into her mother's arms. "Mummy," she whispered, "do I have to go to America?"

"Yes, dear," replied Mummy.

"But why, Mummy?" asked Merry. "Don't you and Daddy want me here with you?"

"Well, you see, darling, Aunt Helen and Uncle Bill haven't any little girl and Daddy and I want to share our little girl with them."

"But you won't have any little girl while I am in America," said Merry.

"It won't be long, dear," said Mummy. "You will be back almost before I can say 'Jack Robinson.' What a lot you will have to tell Daddy and me."

Merry was quiet a long time. Mummy thought

she was asleep but Merry was thinking. After a while she said, "Mummy, I'm not going to take Molly to America with me. I'm going to leave her with you to be your little girl."

"Oh, Merry!" said Mummy, hugging her very tight, "how sweet of you to want to leave Molly with me!"

Merry thought again for a long time. She was having a very hard time deciding something. At last she whispered, "I'll leave Greggie, too, if you want him."

"No, dear," replied Mummy, "you must take Greggie with you. I'll be very happy with Molly."

"You'll be very careful not to sit on her or lie on her, won't you?" asked Merry.

"Indeed, I'll be very careful always to notice where she is," replied Mummy.

"That's good," sighed Merry. "I'm really very glad Greggie is going with me." Then she ran her fingers in her mother's soft hair and went to sleep.

The next morning everyone was up very early. Mr. and Mrs. Ramsay were going to take Merry to the boat to go to America.

When Mummy brushed Merry's hair, Merry said, "Molly has golden curls, you know."

"No, I didn't know that Molly has golden curls," said Mummy. "I'm glad you told me. I'll brush them every day while you are away."

When Merry went downstairs to breakfast, her daddy fastened a little chain around her neck. A metal tag hung from the chain. On one side of the tag was Merry's name, her daddy's name, and her address in London. On the other side was the name and address of Merry's uncle Bill in America. "Now you can't get lost," said Daddy.

Merry sat down at the breakfast table. Beside her plate there was a little box. Merry picked up the box and opened it. There was a tiny golden ring. It had a little blue stone in the center and a pearl on each side. "Oh!" said Merry. "Is it for me?"

"Yes," said Mummy. "It is a remembrance present from Daddy and me."

Merry slipped the ring on her finger. "Oh, thank you," she said, "it's beautiful!"

Merry could hardly eat her breakfast for looking at her new ring. She had never had a ring before.

After breakfast Merry said good-bye to Annie,
the cook. "Will you see that Molly has her tea
every afternoon, Annie?" said Merry.

"That I will," said Annie. Annie's eyes were
red and she wiped a tear on her apron.

"What is the matter, Annie?" asked Merry.
"You're crying."

"Oh, 'tis only the onions," she replied. "They
always make me cry when I peel them."

"Come, Merry," called Daddy, "the cab is
waiting."

Annie pushed a little box into Merry's hand.
"There! Gumdrops!" said Annie. "Just a little
going-away present for you."

"Oh, thank you, Annie," said Merry.

Annie watched her as she ran down the front

steps and jumped into the cab. "She's so little," sobbed Annie, "so little to be going away all by herself."

Merry sat between her mummy and daddy. On her lap she held her best doll, Bonnie. Her suitcase was in front with the driver.

In a moment they were off. When they were halfway to the station, Merry suddenly remembered Greggie. "Where's Greggie?" she cried.

"Gracious!" shouted Daddy. "We have forgotten Greggie! I put him in his traveling basket and left him in the kitchen."

Daddy pulled his watch out of his pocket. "We can't go back now," he said. "If we do, we will miss the boat train."

"Oh, Daddy!" cried Merry. "What will I do without Greggie? What will I do!" Tears ran down Merry's cheeks. Mummy put her arm around her and she leaned her head on Mummy's breast. "Don't cry, my pet," said Mummy. "Don't cry, dear."

"Oh, Mummy! Mummy!" she sobbed. "I don't want to go to America without Greggie. What will he do without me?"

Mummy tried to comfort her little girl but Merry cried all the way to the station.

At the station there were crowds of people. Daddy took Merry's suitcase and hurried Merry and her mummy through the crowd. They had to walk a long way to the train. When they reached it, they climbed into one of the little compartments. Soon they were settled for the long journey to the boat. Merry was still crying.

In a few moments the conductor came past and slammed the doors.

"Oh, Greggie!" sobbed Merry. "My little Greggie!"

Suddenly there was a shrill toot of the train whistle. The train started with a jolt. Then it stopped. Daddy lowered the window and looked out. What did he see but Annie running down the platform beside the train. She was puffing and panting. In her hand she carried the basket with Greggie inside.

Mr. Ramsay waved to her. "Here we are, Annie," he shouted. "Here we are!"

Just then the train began to move. Annie rushed up to the window. Mr. Ramsay reached out and grabbed the basket.

"I saw the basket the minute you left," she shouted. "I ran to the corner and jumped in a cab."

Daddy and Merry were both leaning out of the window now. "Oh, thank you, Annie," cried Daddy.

"Thank you, thank you, Annie," shouted Merry.

Merry waved to Annie as long as she could see her. Then she settled down between Mummy and Daddy. She took the basket on her lap and opened it. She patted Greggie's head. Greggie licked her hand. "Oh, Greggie!" said Merry. "I'm so glad you didn't miss the train."

CAROLYN HAYWOOD (1898–1990) was born in Philadelphia and began her career as an artist. She hoped to become a children's book illustrator, but at an editor's suggestion, she began writing stories about the everyday lives of children. The first of those, *"B" Is for Betsy*, was published in 1939, and more than fifty other books followed. One of America's most popular authors for children, Ms. Haywood used many of her own childhood experiences in her novels. "I write for children," she once explained, "because I feel that they need to know what is going on in their world and they can best understand it through stories."